Dear Parents,

Welcome to the Scholastic Reader series. We have taken over 80 years of experience with teachers, parents, and children and put it into a program that is designed to match your child's interests and skills.

Level 1—Short sentences and stories made up of words kids can sound out using their phonics skills and words that are important to remember.

Level 2—Longer sentences and stories with words kids need to know and new "big" words that they will want to know.

Level 3—From sentences to paragraphs to longer stories, these books have large "chunks" of texts and are made up of a rich vocabulary.

Level 4—First chapter books with more words and fewer pictures.

It is important that children learn to read well enough to succeed in school and beyond. Here are ideas for reading this book with your child:

- Look at the book together. Encourage your child to read the title and make a prediction about the story.
- Read the book together. Encourage your child to sound out words when appropriate. When your child struggles, you can help by providing the word.
- Encourage your child to retell the story. This is a great way to check for comprehension.
- Have your child take the fluency test on the last page to check progress.

Scholastic Readers are designed to support your child's efforts to learn how to read at every age and every stage. Enjoy helping your child learn to read and love to read.

—**Francie Alexande**
Chief Education Off
Scholastic Education

D1056882

For our little princesses, Dariyah and Sakinah
—S.W.B.

For Jerry
—B.L.

ISBN 0-439-47154-0

Text copyright © 2003 by Scholastic.
Illustrations copyright © 2003 by Barbara Lanza.
All rights reserved. Published by Scholastic Inc.
SCHOLASTIC, CARTWHEEL BOOKS, and associated logos are trademarks
and/or registered trademarks of Scholastic Inc.

Library of Congress Cataloging-in-Publication Data available.

10 9 8 7 6 5 4 3   05 06 07

Printed in the U.S.A. 23 • First printing, September 2003

Little Mermaid

by **Sonia W. Black**

Illustrated by **Barbara Lanza**

Scholastic Reader — Level 2

SCHOLASTIC INC. Cartwheel ·B·O·O·K·S·®

New York Toronto London Auckland Sydney
Mexico City New Delhi Hong Kong Buenos Aires

The Sea King had six daughters.
Little Mermaid was the youngest
and most beautiful.

All day, the princesses had fun together.
At night, they enjoyed their grandmother's
stories about the Upper World.
They longed to go above and see it.

But Grandmother said,
"You must be fifteen years old first."
Little Mermaid had to wait her turn.

At last, Little Mermaid went
above with her sisters.
The princesses played and sang all day.
Little Mermaid had the best voice of all.

One day, Little Mermaid
swam above alone.

She saw
a big ship with
a handsome young
prince on the deck.

Little Mermaid
fell in love.

Suddenly, a great storm came.
The prince was drowning.
Little Mermaid saved him.

She waited till he woke up.

Then she swam home sadly.
"I want to be human and
marry the prince," she said.
"The Sea Witch will help me."

The Sea Witch made a magic drink.

"This will make you human.

You will have legs.

But they will hurt!" she warned.

"And if the prince marries someone

else, you will turn to sea foam!"

Then she said, "In return for my magic drink, I must take your lovely voice!"

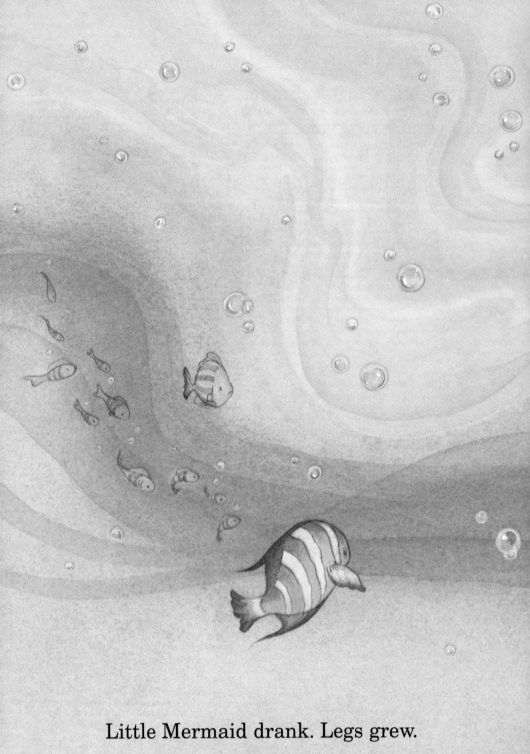

Little Mermaid drank. Legs grew.
She felt sharp pain and fainted.

When she awoke, she
saw the handsome prince.
"You are so beautiful!"
he said.

Little Mermaid tried
to speak. No words
came out!

"Come home with me,"
said the prince.
Her legs hurt with
every step.

Little Mermaid and the prince
spent happy times together.
She could not speak.
But, in pain, she danced for him!

All the while, she thought
about marrying him.

But one day, Little Mermaid
heard the prince would marry
someone else.

She remembered the witch's spell.
I will turn to sea foam,
she thought, sadly.

The prince and the beautiful princess
had a big wedding.

Could Little
Mermaid break
the witch's spell
before morning?

Her sisters came.
They gave her a knife
from the Sea Witch.

"You must kill the prince tonight.
Then you will be like us again!" they said.

But Little Mermaid could not do it.
She kissed the prince good-bye.

At sunrise, Little Mermaid dove into the sea.
She turned into sea foam,
forever dancing with the waves.

Fluency Fun

The words in each list below end in the same sounds.
Read the words in a list.
Read them again.
Read them faster.
Try to read all 15 words in one minute.

pain	**leak**	**night**
brain	**bleak**	**bright**
train	**creak**	**fright**
strain	**speak**	**delight**
remain	**squeak**	**tonight**

Look for these words in the story.

beautiful   together   above

human   thought

Note to Parents:

According to *A Dictionary of Reading and Related Terms*, fluency is "the ability to read smoothly, easily, and readily with freedom from word-recognition problems." Fluency is necessary for good comprehension and enjoyable reading. The activities on this page include a speed drill and a sight-recognition drill. Speed drills build fluency because they help students rapidly recognize common syllables and spelling patterns in words, and they're fun! Sight-recognition drills help students smoothly and accurately recognize words. Practice these activities with your child to help him or her become a fluent reader.

—**Wiley Blevins,**
Reading Specialist